Captain Mama's Surprise

La Sorpresa de Capitán Mamá

By Graciela Tiscareño-Sato • Illustrated by Linda Lens

Gracefully Global Group

Hayward, California

No part of this book may be reproduced or transmitted in any form or by any means, electronic or mechanical, including photocopying, recording, or by any information storage and retrieval system, without permission in writing from the publisher.

Copyright © 2016 by Graciela Tiscareño-Sato. All rights reserved.

Published by Gracefully Global Group, LLC, 22568 Mission Blvd, No. 427, Hayward, California 94541. GracefullyGlobal.com.

Cataloging Data

Tiscareño-Sato, Graciela.

Captain Mama's Surprise / La Sorpresa de Capitán Mamá / by Graciela Tiscareño-Sato: Illustrated by Linda Lens

Summary: In this second book in the Captain Mama series, Marco and his sisters, whose mother is a U.S. Air Force aviator, visit the KC-135 aerial refueling tanker on a field trip with his second grade class. The children and their teachers meet the aircrew and the crew chief, tour the airplane to understand its unique parts and learn what each crew member does as they work together onboard this gas station in the sky. Includes a STEM activity for children to learn basic aircraft terms and structure.

ISBN: 978-0-9973090-0-3 (paperback)
ISBN: 978-0-9973090-3-4 (Hardcover)
ISBN: 978-0-9973090-1-0 (Kindle)
ISBN: 978-0-9973090-2-7 (iBook version in iTunes)

Library of Congress Control Number: 2016904918

Library of Congress Subject Headings
[1. Bilingual – Easy Picture. 2. Women air pilots – Fiction. 3. Air pilots, Military – Fiction.
4. Hispanic American women -- Juvenile literature. 5. United States. -- Air Force -- Fiction.]

Book design: Suzi Lee Musgrove, SLM Creative Design and Associates, Novato, CA. www.slmcreative.com

Inquiries for Author/Illustrator visits (in person & via Skype): info@GracefullyGlobal.com or call (510) 542-9449.
Teacher Packs (books and embroidered patches) and author-signed books available via GracefullyGlobal.com/Commerce.

Printed in the United States. First printing, Spring 2016.

All URLs in this book were valid at press time. However, due to the dynamic nature of the Internet, some addresses may have changed or sites may have changed or ceased to exist since publication. While the author and publisher regret any inconvenience this may cause readers, no responsibility for any such changes can be accepted by either the author or the publisher.

I dedicate this book to Gabriel and Peyton who each lost a parent aboard Shell 77 in Kyrgyzstan on May 3, 2013 and to Jacob at Akers Elementary School at NAS Lemoore. On a school visit there, Jacob told me of his father's passing shortly after his fourth tour in Iraq. You three represent to me all children who have lost a parent who voluntarily served in our armed forces. We can only salute you and thank you for your unwilling sacrifice made on our behalf. We will keep your mothers and fathers alive through stories, written and verbal, so that they will never be forgotten. More than anyone, you know that our freedom is NOT free.

- Graciela

For my darling kids, Johnny and Saila: May you always soar to meet your goals and overcome the challenges that life will bring! For Danny: you've been more help than I could have ever imagined. For my wonderful parents who've been by my side this whole time. For those of you reading this who have ever made me laugh (really LAUGH): this is for you too, because the happier I am, the more creative is my soul! xoxoxoxox.

- Linda

Table of Contents

Story text 4-33

Glossary (English) 34

Glosario (Spanish) 35

Educational Resources 36

Art/Engineering Project 37

Acknowledgements 38

Thanks to earliest supporters 39

Book endorsements 40

Standing on the step of the bus exit, I see it—the big flying gas station where my mom works! I pull my hood on as the rain starts to hit me. There's the American flag painted on the tail! In my pocket I feel the flag patch I still love to stick on my pajamas. It's one of the patches Mama gave me when I was little.

I can't wait to show my mom off to my friends! They're yelling at me to get off the bus, eager to get inside the plane. When my parents took us to school earlier, Mama said, "See you at the jet, Marco!" Could she be more excited than me about this field trip?

There's my big sister Mimi next to Mama, waving as Mama attaches a ladder to the airplane and climbs up.

AMC
80050

Estoy parado en el escalón de la puerta del autobús escolar, y veo la gran gasolinera voladora donde trabaja mi mamá. Me pongo mi capucha cuando siento que cae la lluvia. ¡Allí está la bandera americana pintada en la cola del avión! En mi bolsillo toco el parche de la bandera que aún le pongo a mis pijamas. Es uno de los parches que me regaló mamá cuando estaba pequeñito.

¡Estoy tan orgulloso que mis amigos conozcan a mi mamá! Me están gritando que me baje del autobús, ansiosos de subirse al avión. Al dejarnos en la escuela antes de ir a trabajar, mamá me dijo —¡Te veo en el avión Marco!—¿Me pregunto si ella está más entusiasmada que yo?

Allí está mi hermana mayor Mimí con mamá, saludándome mientras mamá pone la escalera al avión y se sube.

That's my signal! With my teacher, Ms. Winblad, I lead my class and soon I'm climbing the ladder. I stop halfway and look up as Mimi steps off and into the plane's flight deck. Mama smiles down at me and I climb up as fast as I can!

Behind me, I hear "Wow, this is cool!" as my friend David climbs up. My whole second-grade class is going to climb up, just like real aircrew members.

¡Ésa es la señal! Con mi maestra, la señora Winblad, encaminamos a mis compañeros y en un dos por tres ya estamos en la escalera. Me paro a la mitad y miro hacia arriba mientras que Mimí termina de subir y se mete a la cabina de vuelo. ¡Mamá me mira y sonríe mientras que subo lo más rápido que puedo!

Atrás de mí escucho —¡Wow qué asombroso!—mientras sube mi amigo Davíd. Todos los de mi clase del segundo año van a subir tal cual como verdaderos miembros de la tripulación.

On the flight deck, my mom hugs me and greets my friends. She tells everyone to step into the back part of the plane. Miss Calderon, our other teacher, is there, gathering kids like a mother duck with her ducklings. She touches our heads, counting that we're all there.

"Welcome to the KC-135 Aerial Refueling Tanker," says my Captain Mama with a big smile. "Marco and I have been looking forward to bringing you out to the plane!" she says, ruffling my hair.

Ya estando en la cabina de vuelo, mi mamá me abraza y saluda a mis amigos. Les dice a todos que pasen al lado trasero del avión. Nuestra otra maestra, la señorita Calderón, está allí juntando a los niños como una pata junta a sus patitos y nos cuenta para asegurarse que todos estemos allí.

—Bienvenidos al Avión Tanquero KC-135—dice mi Capitán Mamá con una gran sonrisa. —¡Marco y yo teníamos muchas ganas de traerlos al avión!—dice ella—despeinándome.

"Please turn around and meet the pilots who just joined us: Captain Vicky Castro, the aircraft commander who sits in the left seat and Lieutenant Kai Tanabe is our copilot who sits in the right seat," she says.

"This is our crew chief, Sergeant Sergio. He makes sure everything works on this airplane. Every jet has its own crew chief." Sergeant Sergio waves and says, "Welcome to my baby! I'm excited to show her to you."

—Por favor dense la vuelta y saluden a los pilotos que acaban de llegar—dice mamá. —Les presento a la Capitán Vicky Castro, la comandante del avión que se sienta en el asiento izquierdo. Por aquí tenemos al Teniente Kai Tanabe, nuestro copiloto que se sienta en el asiento derecho—dice ella.

—Éste es nuestro jefe mecánico, el Sargento Sergio—continúa Mamá. —Él se encarga de que todo esté bien en el avión. Cada avión tiene su propio jefe mecánico.

—¡Bienvenidos a mi nave!—nos saluda el Sargento. —Me da mucho gusto que estén aquí.

"Meet Sergeant Christy, our boom operator," Mama continues, as a lady walks towards us from the back of the plane.

"Welcome to my office," says the sergeant.

My mom continues, "Today you'll meet the crew and see different parts of the plane. You'll learn why there are four aircrew members and what each of us does to fly this gas station."

....

Veo una mujer acercándose a nosotros. —Allí viene la Sargenta Christy, la operadora de la pértiga—continúa Mamá.

—Bienvenidos a mi oficina—dice la sargenta.

Mamá continúa—Ahora ustedes conocerán a la tripulación y verán las diferentes partes del avión. Aprenderán por qué hay cuatro miembros en la tripulación y lo que hace cada uno para volar esta gasolinera.

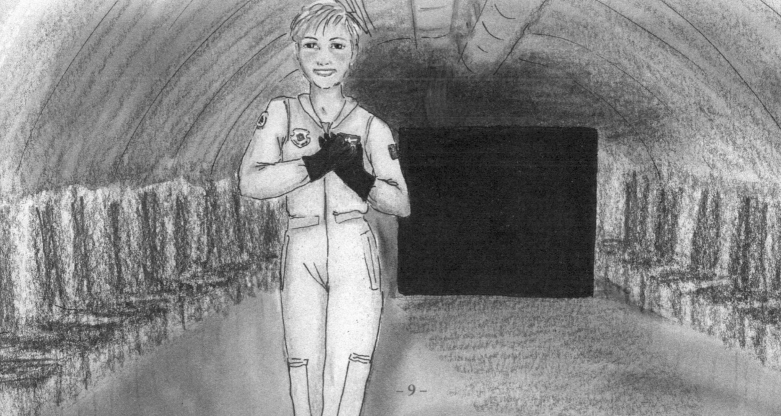

Mom waves to Ms. Winblad and our teacher counts several students, including me and my two best friends, Kiyoshi and Adriana. "Sergeant Christy, please take Ms. Winblad's group to the boom pod."

"Yes, ma'am," replies Sergeant Christy. "Walk this way, kids!" she says. We follow her to the back of the jet.

Mamá saluda a la señora Winblad. Nuestra maestra cuenta varios estudiantes, incluyéndome a mí y a mis dos mejores amigos, Kiyoshi y Adriana. —Sargenta Christy, por favor lleve al grupo de la Señora Winblad a la cabina del operador de la pértiga.

—Sí señora—responde la Sargenta Christy. —Caminen por acá niños—dice ella. La seguimos hasta el fondo del avión.

I hear my mom say, "Ms. Calderon and Mimi, please take your group to Sergeant Sergio by the over-wing window. Everybody else, please follow me and Keiko, Marco's other sister, up to the flight deck."

My teacher and oldest sister Mimi lead my friends back; my ten year-old sister Keiko and my mom walk up front.

Mamá dice—Señorita Calderón y Mimí, por favor lleven su grupo a la ventana sobre el ala donde está el Sargento Sergio. Los demás, por favor síganos a mí y a Keiko, la otra hermana de Marco, a la cabina de vuelo.

Mi maestra y mi hermana mayor Mimí dirigen a mis amigos hacia atrás y mi hermana Keiko de diez años y mi mamá caminan hacia el frente.

The first thing I notice in the back are the rows of yellow metal tanks.

"Are these bombs?" Kiyoshi asks, gently touching the tanks and reading my mind.

"What an interesting question," Sergeant Christy replies. "They're not bombs; they're oxygen tanks so we can breathe when we fly."

Lo primero que noto en la parte de atrás son todos los tanques amarillos.

—¿Estas son bombas?—pregunta Kiyoshi, tocando los tanques delicadamente y leyéndome la mente.

—Qué pregunta tan interesante—responde la Sargenta Christy.
—No son bombas. Son tanques de oxígeno para poder respirar cuando estemos en el aire.

Sergeant Christy asks Kiyoshi and Adriana to step down into the space below the floor, left of the oxygen tanks. She tells them to lay on their stomachs, then she steps down on the right side. She looks up at me and says, "Follow me, Marco."

What a tiny space I'm in! I'm on my stomach just like Sergeant Christy. She's in the middle between my friends and me. The ceiling almost touches our heads.

La Sargenta Christy le pide a Kiyoshi y Adriana que bajen al espacio debajo del piso, al lado izquierdo de los tanques. Les dice que se acuesten boca abajo y luego ella se baja al lado derecho. Voltea hacia arriba y me dice—¡Sígueme Marco!

¡Estoy dentro de un espacio tan pequeño! Estoy acostado boca abajo igual que la Sargenta Christy. Ella está entre mis amigos y yo. Nuestras cabezas casi topan con el techo.

"Welcome to the business end of the plane, the part we call the boom pod. The boom is the long pipe with little wings that we use to pass gas from our airplane's gas tanks to another airplane as we fly."

"Pass gas. That's funny," Kiyoshi snickers. Adriana rolls her eyes.

"I thought you'd like that," Sergeant Christy says, smiling. "It's my job to connect us safely to the other plane."

—Bienvenidos a la parte divertida del avión, la parte que le llamamos la cabina del operador de la pértiga—dice la Sargenta Christy. —La pértiga es la pipa larga con alas pequeñas que usamos para echar gasolina o como se dice, pasar gas, de nuestro avión a otro avión mientras estamos en vuelo.

—Pasar gas. ¡Qué chistoso!—dice Kiyoshi con una risita. Adriana voltea sus ojos hacia arriba sarcásticamente.

—Sabía que les gustaría eso—dice la Sargenta Christy sonriendo. —Mi trabajo es conectar la pértiga de manera segura al otro avión.

"This is cool. There's a joystick back here!" Adriana observes.

"Yep, it sure looks like one, doesn't it?" Sergeant Christy replies. "I use this control to fly the boom around when we're in the air. These are the three most important gauges I look at: they tell me how far side to side the boom is, how long it is and how far up or down it is. If the pilot of the plane we are refueling moves around too much, I disconnect the boom to keep us safe."

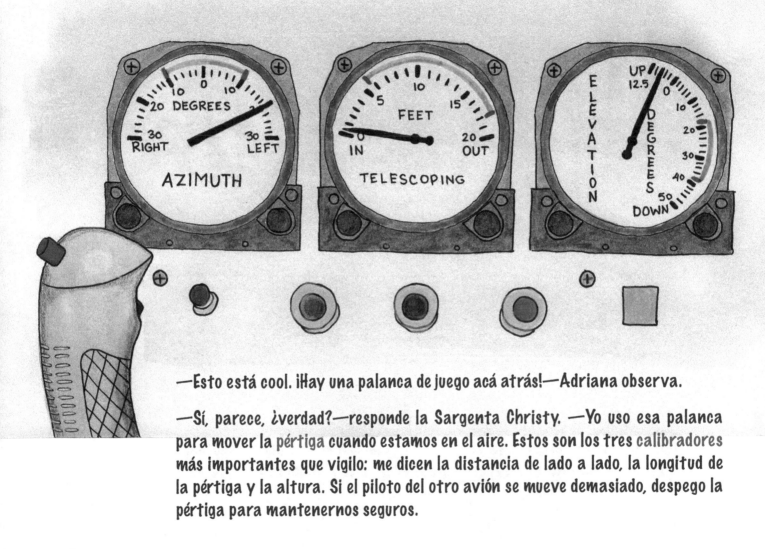

—Esto está cool. ¡Hay una palanca de juego acá atrás!—Adriana observa.

—Sí, parece, ¿verdad?—responde la Sargenta Christy. —Yo uso esa palanca para mover la pértiga cuando estamos en el aire. Estos son los tres calibradores más importantes que vigilo: me dicen la distancia de lado a lado, la longitud de la pértiga y la altura. Si el piloto del otro avión se mueve demasiado, despego la pértiga para mantenernos seguros.

"Is it scary to connect to another airplane when flying?" I ask.

"No, it's not scary because I've been trained for many hours to do this," replies the sergeant. "I'm trained for emergencies, too. There's no need for fear when you've learned to do something well."

—¿Le da miedo conectar un avión a otro avión mientras esta en vuelo? —le pregunto.

—No. No me da miedo porque me he preparado muchas horas para hacer esto—responde la sargenta. —También me he preparado para emergencias. No hay necesidad de tener miedo cuando has aprendido hacer las cosas bien.

"How far away is the other airplane when you're connected to it?" Kiyoshi asks.

"Usually, I am between 36 and 48 feet from the other plane," she answers. "The boom itself is 28 feet long and I can extend it up to 19 feet during aerial refueling."

—¿A qué distancia está el otro avión cuando se conectan a él?—pregunta Kiyoshi.

—Normalmente yo estoy entre 36 y 48 pies de distancia—ella contesta.
—La pértiga mide 28 pies de largo y la puedo extender otros 19 pies cuando estamos pasándole gasolina al otro avión.

"Do you like working here?" I ask.

"It's the coolest job in the world," she tells us. "I open my window and see a military plane coming up for fuel. Can't do a mission without gas, right?"

—¿Le gusta trabajar aquí?—le pregunto.

—Es el trabajo más divertido del mundo—nos dice ella. —Abro la ventana y veo un avión militar subiendo para echarle gasolina. No se puede hacer una misión sin gasolina, ¿verdad?

"I wish I could see you do that," Adriana says. "It must be amazing."

"Maybe someday you will," replies the boom operator. "Wishes sometimes come true. Are you ready to go to the flight deck?"

"Yeah, let's do it!" we exclaim.

—Sueño con poder verla hacer eso—dice Adriana. —Debe ser asombroso.

—Quizás un día podrás—responde la operadora de la pértiga. —Los sueños se hacen realidad. ¿Están listos para ir a la cabina de vuelo?

—Sí, ¡vamos!—exclamamos.

We crawl out of the tiny boom pod. We walk past Ms. Calderon, Sergeant Sergio and our friends. They're doing something with a red crank in the floor. I hear Sergeant Sergio say "... just in case the landing gear doesn't come down."

....

Salimos gateando de la cabina pequeña. Pasamos por frente de la Señora Calderón, el Sargento Sergio y nuestros amigos. Ellos están haciendo algo con una manivela roja en el piso. Escucho al Sargento Sergio decir—...en caso de que no baje el tren de aterrizaje.

We enter the flight deck and my mom smiles at us. "Welcome back, kids! Come in."

I squeeze in near my mom and the copilot seat; my friends are all around us.

....

Entramos a la cabina de vuelo y mamá nos sonríe. —¡Bienvenidos otra vez niños! ¡Pasen!

Me paro cerca de mi mamá y el asiento del copiloto. Mis amigos nos rodean.

Captain Castro, the pilot in the left seat, says, "Hi everybody! I'm the senior pilot on the crew, the aircraft commander. I'm in charge of this plane, crew and mission every time we fly. I've been flying this plane for over six years and have over 2500 flight hours. This is Lieutenant Kai Tanabe, my copilot. Together with our navigator, we are the officers on the crew. We work with our boom operator to fly this plane and get the mission done on time and safely."

La Capitán Castro, el piloto en el asiento izquierdo, dice—¡Hola a todos! Soy la encargada de este avión, de la tripulación y de la misión cada vez que volamos. He volado este avión por más de seis años y tengo más de 2500 horas de vuelo. Él es el Teniente Kai Tanabe, mi copiloto. Junto con nuestra navegadora, somos los oficiales de la tripulación. Trabajamos con la operadora de la pértiga para volar este avión y completar la misión a tiempo y de manera segura.

Kiyoshi blurts out, "Excuse me, where's the fuel stored on the plane? How does it get to the boom?"

Kiyoshi no se puede contener y pregunta—Disculpe ¿Dónde está el combustible en este avión? ¿Cómo llega a la pértiga?

Lieutenant Tanabe explains, "The ten fuel tanks are in both wings and under your feet. During the refueling part of the flight, our boom operator tells us when we're connected to the other airplane. We can't see what's going on back there—no rearview mirrors! When Sergeant Christy says, 'Contact,' I look here at this button and confirm we're connected to the receiver plane."

El Teniente Tanabe explica—Los diez tanques de combustible se encuentran en las dos alas y debajo de sus pies. Cuando estamos en el aire, nuestra operadora de la pértiga nos dice cuando estamos conectados al receptor. No podemos ver lo que está sucediendo allá atrás...¡no hay retrovisores! Cuando la Sargenta Christy dice—Contacto—miro este botón y confirmo que estamos conectados al otro avión.

"I push these switches to get our fuel to flow from our tanks to the boom and into the other plane," he continues. "My job as copilot includes doing take offs and landings, managing our fuel system and keeping the plane balanced."

—Presiono estos botoncitos para conseguir que la gasolina fluya de nuestros tanques a la pértiga y al otro avión—él continua. —Mi trabajo como copiloto incluye hacer los despegues, los aterrizajes, y la gestión de nuestro sistema de combustible y mantener el avión equilibrado.

My mom turns sideways in her seat and continues, "We use these headsets to talk to each other inside the plane because it's really loud when we're flying. My station includes radar controls so we can avoid bad weather and navigation systems to get us where we need to go. With these systems and fast mental math, I keep our mission on time so we can refuel planes anywhere in the world.

Mi mamá voltea su silla hacia un lado y continúa—Usamos estos audífonos para comunicarnos el uno con el otro adentro del avión porque hay mucho ruido cuando estamos volando. Mi estación incluye los controles del radar para evitar tormentas, y los sistemas de navegación que nos llevan a donde vamos. Con estos sistemas y cálculos mentales rápidos, mantengo nuestra misión a tiempo para que podamos trabajar en cualquier parte del mundo.

"These special charts help us to always know where our plane is over the Earth," she said, holding up a colorful chart with mountains, oceans, rivers and many lines, numbers and words. It looked nothing like the maps we have in our car.

—Estos diagramas especiales nos ayudan a saber siempre en qué parte del planeta está nuestro avión—dice ella, levantado un diagrama colorido con montañas, océanos, ríos y muchas líneas, números y palabras. No se parecía nada a los mapas que teníamos en nuestro carro.

I ask Captain Castro, "Is it scary to be the one in charge?"

"It's not scary," she tells me. "It's a big responsibility, yes. I love to be the leader of this excellent crew. I've loved everything about jets since I was a little girl just like your mother. This is a special airplane and a cool job."

Le pregunto a la Capitán Castro
—¿Le da miedo ser la encargada?

—No me da miedo—me responde ella. —Pero sí es una gran responsabilidad. Me gusta ser la líder de esta excelente tripulación. Todo de los aviones me ha fascinado desde que era niña, igual que a tu mamá. Éste es un avión especial y me encanta.

"Ready to go back to Sergeant Sergio?" my mom asks.

We turn to leave the flight deck and notice the lights are out in the back.

—¿Están listos para volver con el Sargento Sergio?—pregunta mamá.

Nos volteamos para irnos de la cabina de vuelo y notamos que las luces de la parte de atrás están apagadas.

As we walk out of the flight deck, my mother turns on the cabin lights. That's when I see our backpacks hanging on the seats!

Al momento de salir de la cabina de vuelo, mamá prende las luces de la cabina. ¡Es cuando veo nuestras mochilas colgadas de los asientos del avión!

"Surprise! Today isn't just a field trip to see the jet—we're going to take you all flying!" my mom says excitedly.

—¡Sorpresa! Hoy no solo es una excursión para ver el avión—¡vamos a volar!
—dice mamá gustosa.

I feel my jaw drop and look around.

David says "What?! Really?"

"Yeah, alright!" yells Kiyoshi, as he jumps and pumps his fist in the air.
"Woo-hoo!" says Adriana as she hugs me. "I can't believe this! My first airplane ride!"

....

Me quedo boquiabierto.

Davíd dice —¡¿Qué?! ¿De verdad?

—Sí, ¡qué emoción!—grita Kiyoshi, brincando y levantando sus brazos hacia arriba.
—¡Wow!—dice Adriana dándome un abrazo. —¡No lo puedo creer! ¡Mi primer vuelo en avión!

"Is it true, Mama?" I ask, still in shock, feeling my eyes open wide.

"Yes, it is true, sweetheart," she replies with a wide grin and a hug. "Go back and strap into your seat. Our adventure is about to begin!"

—¿Es cierto, Mamá?—le pregunto conmocionado, con mis ojos casi saliéndose de mis órbitas.

—Claro que sí cariño—me responde con una gran sonrisa y un abrazo. —Ve, siéntate, y amárrate el cinturón. ¡Nuestra aventura está por comenzar!

Glossary

Flight deck – the front part of an airplane where the crew pilots the plane

Refueling tanker – a special type of military airplane that passes fuel from its tanks to other military planes in flight. Today's U.S. Air Force flies KC-135s and KC-10s. Soon a new tanker will join the fleet, the KC-46. To see video of its first test flight in September 2015, search Boeing's KC-46A Pegasus Completes Successful First Test Flight on YouTube. Will YOU fly the new tanker?

Captain – The third military officer rank, usually received after four years of service as a Lieutenant. See all commissioned officer rank insignia at defense.gov/About-DoD/Insignias/Officers. Learn about Air Force pay grades at airforce.com/careers/pay-and-benefits.

Lieutenant – The first and second of the military officer ranks. A new officer starts as a Second Lieutenant (2LT) after graduating from a four-year university or a military academy. After two years of service, a 2LT is promoted to First Lieutenant (1LT), the rank on Lieutenant Tanabe's shoulders.

Crew chief – a highly-trained airman usually assigned to an airplane to make sure everything is working on the plane

Sergeant – a leadership rank in the enlisted force. See all enlisted rank insignia at: defense.gov/About-DoD/Insignias/Enlisted. Learn about Air Force pay grades at airforce.com/careers/pay-and-benefits.

Boom operator – crew member whose job it is to safely connect the boom to the refueling system of the other plane in flight

Boom pod – the small area at the back of the plane where the boom operator controls the refueling boom system

Boom – long metal tube at the back of the tanker that attaches to the receiving plane. The outer tube of the boom is 28 feet long; the inner tube is 19 feet long and extends out. Small wings on the boom allow it to be "flown" around by the boom operator.

Gauges – displays for crewmembers to receive important information about how the plane's systems are working

Landing gear – the tires and wheels under the airplane that touch the ground first when a plane lands. These fold up into the plane after the plane takes off.

Officers – Ranking service members who have graduated from college or a military academy before entering the military. Officers are usually in positions of leadership. Pilots Captain Castro, Lt. Tanabe and Captain Mama are all officers.

Receiver – the plane that connects to a tanker to get fuel

Radar – a system on the plane used to see objects outside the plane when flying. The crew uses it to learn how far away, and in what direction, something is (like thunderstorms or other airplanes) from the tanker.

Navigation – A mathematical process used to know where you are and where you're going next. The crew uses the plane's current location, speed, direction it's pointing, wind speed and other things to know where to fly and how fast to do the refueling mission on time and in the right place.

Glosario

Cabina de vuelo – la parte de enfrente del avión en donde la tripulación se encarga de volar el avión

Avión tanquero – un tipo de avión militar especial que pasa combustible de sus tanques a otros aviones militares en vuelo. La Fuerza Aérea Estadounidense de hoy vuela KC-135s y KC-10s. Pronto se unirá otro tanquero nuevo a la flota, el KC-46. Para ver el video de su primer vuelo de prueba en septiembre del 2015, busque Boeing's KC-46A Pegasus Completes Successful First Test Flight en YouTube. ¿USTED volará en el tanquero nuevo?

Capitán – El tercer grado militar, normalmente recibido después de cuatro años de servicio como Teniente. Vea todos los rangos militares para los oficiales en: defense.gov/About-DoD/Insignias/Officers. Aprenda acerca de los niveles de pago de la Fuerza Aérea en: airforce.com/careers/pay-and-benefits.

Teniente – El primer y el segundo grado para los oficiales militares. Un oficial nuevo empieza como Segundo Teniente (2Tte.) después de recibirse de una universidad de cuatro años o de una academia militar. Después de dos años de servicio, un 2Tte. asciende a Primer Teniente (1Tte.), el grado en los hombros del Tte. Tanabe.

Jefe mecánico – un mecánico especializado normalmente asignado a un avión para asegurarse de que todo esté funcionando en orden en el avión

Sargento – un grado de liderazgo en la fuerza alistada. Vea todas las insignias de grados alistados en: defense.gov/About-DoD/Insignias/Enlisted. Aprenda acerca de los niveles de pago de la Fuerza Aérea en: airforce.com/careers/pay-and-benefits.

Operador/a de la pértiga – un miembro de la tripulación cuyo trabajo es conectar la pértiga de manera segura al sistema de reabastecimiento del otro avión, en vuelo

Cabina del operador de la pértiga – un área pequeña en el fondo del avión en donde el operador de la pértiga controla el sistema de reabastecimiento con la pértiga

Pértiga – tubo de metal largo en el fondo del tanquero que se pega al avión receptor. El tubo exterior de la pértiga mide 28 pies de largo; el tubo interior mide 19 pies de largo y se extiende. Las alas pequeñas en la pértiga permiten que el operador de la pértiga la haga "volar" por todos lados.

Calibradores – monitores para que los miembros de la tripulación reciban información importante acerca de cómo están funcionando los sistemas del avión

Tren de aterrizaje – las llantas debajo del avión que son necesarias para el aterrizaje. Estas se guardan hacia adentro del avión después del despegue del avión.

Oficiales – Grado de los miembros del servicio militar que se han graduado de la universidad o de una academia militar antes de entrar a las fuerzas armadas. Los oficiales suelen estar en posiciones de liderazgo. Los pilotos Capitán Castro, Teniente Tanabe, y Capitán Mamá todos son oficiales.

Receptor – el avión que se conecta al tanquero para recibir combustible

Radar – un instrumento utilizado para detectar objetos / aviones cerca durante el vuelo. La tripulación lo usa para saber qué tan lejos y en qué dirección está algo (como las tormentas eléctricas u otros aviones) del tanquero.

Navegación – Un proceso matemático usado para saber en dónde estás y a dónde vas en todo momento. La tripulación usa el lugar actual del avión, la velocidad, la dirección en la que apunta, la velocidad del aire y otras cosas para saber hacia dónde volar y que tan rápido hacer la misión de reabastecimiento a tiempo y en el lugar correcto.

Educational Resources

Learn more about airplanes, free orientation flights, aerial refueling, women veterans and more

Young Eagles® Flight Program – Free orientation flight to see what pilots do on the ground and in the air, for kids between the ages of 8 and 17. Google Young Eagles Find a Flight and you'll find the site at the eaa.org domain.

Civil Air Patrol – A nonprofit organization and auxiliary of the U.S. Air Force established by Congress in 1948. To become a CAP cadet, you must be at least 12 years old and not yet 19 years old. Find a local squadron with your zip code with unit locator at GoCivilAirPatrol.com.

Women Of Aviation Worldwide Week – WOAW is a global outreach initiative that takes place annually during the week of March 8, the anniversary date of the world's first female pilot license since 1910 and International Women's Day since 1914. Girls and women can sign up for FREE orientation flights at this time.

Visit womenofaviationweek.org to find local events and flight opportunities. The WOAW website is now available in Spanish.

Hispanic Association of Aviation and Aerospace Professionals (HAAAP) – Are you near San Antonio, Texas? HAAAP inspires Latino students and young adults to seek civilian and military aviation careers, by taking them on detailed airport surveys, where they tour various airplanes and control towers. Connect by searching group name on Facebook.

Official Boeing (aircraft manufacturer) page dedicated to the history and technical specifications of the KC-135: boeing.com/history/products/kc-135-stratotanker.page

Official 92nd Air Refueling Wing at Fairchild Air Force Base (FAFB) site – Author was stationed at FAFB from 1992 to 1999. Read base history and highlights of military operations she participated in with her fellow KC-135 crew members at fairchild.af.mil/library/factsheets/factsheet.asp?id=3769

Videos: There are many cool refueling videos on YouTube. Here are two channels the author enjoys and recommends:
1) Anthony Burleson –USAF KC-135R pilot has shared a terrific collection of refueling videos he created during his military career, including the Air Force demonstration team, the Thunderbirds, refueling. youtube.com/user/AnthonyBurleson
2) Gung Ho Vids – (refueling plus LOTS of other videos from both inside and outside jets, and other military systems... all in HD.) On YouTube search Gung Ho Vids.

Women Veteran Speakers.com – the first, national speakers' bureau comprised entirely of women who have served in our nation's armed forces. Great resource for educators and event organizers around the nation to connect with women veterans from ALL military branches. Speakers are available for school assemblies and classroom visits for Women's History Month, Veterans Day, Memorial Day and more. Learn about military life from women! womenveteranspeakers.com.

ART/ENGINEERING PROJECT (copy this page)

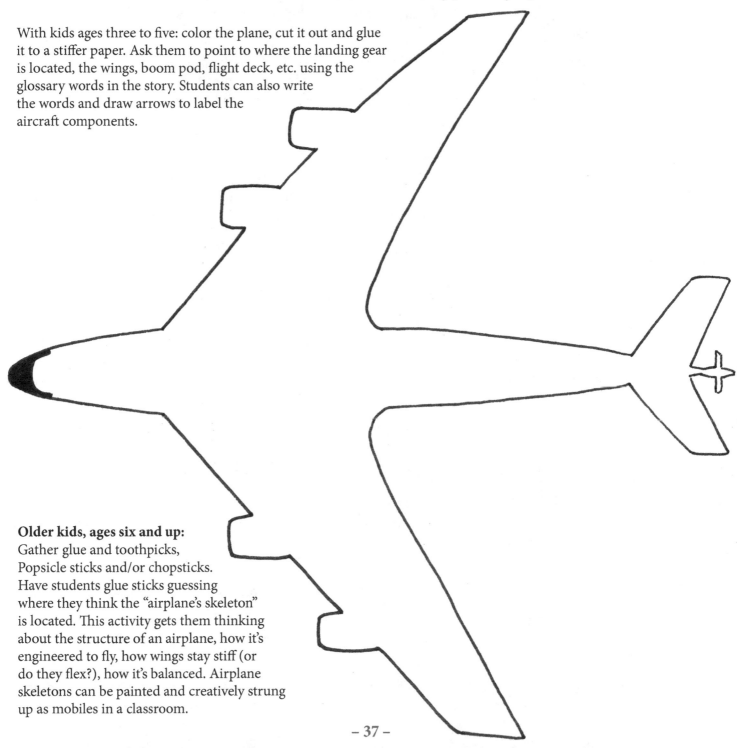

With kids ages three to five: color the plane, cut it out and glue it to a stiffer paper. Ask them to point to where the landing gear is located, the wings, boom pod, flight deck, etc. using the glossary words in the story. Students can also write the words and draw arrows to label the aircraft components.

Older kids, ages six and up:
Gather glue and toothpicks, Popsicle sticks and/or chopsticks. Have students glue sticks guessing where they think the "airplane's skeleton" is located. This activity gets them thinking about the structure of an airplane, how it's engineered to fly, how wings stay stiff (or do they flex?), how it's balanced. Airplane skeletons can be painted and creatively strung up as mobiles in a classroom.

Acknowledgements of Gratitude

Vicky Cepeda – for providing critical input early on, thinking like the mother of a young boy, suggesting little Marco become the storyteller.

Linda Lens – for expertly creating the beautiful images that make this book (and series) possible. Also, for telling me to SLOW DOWN. Thanks for urging me to take the children through the different parts of this unique airplane after your first visit to a KC-135R, before the story goes airborne in book #3.

Kerrin Torres–Meriwether – veteran, mother and teacher - for her early reading of the manuscript when it was way too much and for also helping me to slow down.

The Air Force Book Support Team in New York, the 349th Air Mobility Wing Public Affairs staff at Travis AFB and the transiting aircrew from McConnell AFB – for all the help getting illustrator Linda her first-ever experience on a KC-135R. That precious hour was critical to her understanding of why I love this plane.

Teachers Patti Brohard, Virginia Winblad and Lisa Calderon – my children's effective, loving teachers who inspired the characters along for the adventure.

Anabel Granados – for the research time spent learning obscure military aviation words, translating everthing into Spanish and for "thinking like a little boy" to give voice to Marco, our storyteller.

Jonathon Pece and Christy Schultz – my friends and former KC-135R aircrew members who I spent time with up in the air, in the United Kingdom, Saudi Arabia, Turkey and on ski slopes. Thank you for being my go-to friends for technical support. Thank you **Ray Lewis**, boom operator, who while deployed to Turkey, provided photos to assist the illustrator.

Justine Cromer, who I met as Captain Tanabe – for being my sponsor when I arrived at my first squadron and for becoming my dear friend for life.

My parents, Arturo and Agustina Tiscareño – for insisting I speak Spanish daily as a child AND for serving as first-round editors of the Spanish translation.

Rosi Bustamante – for further enhancing the Spanish text with the voice of a young child as only a bilingual, bicultural mother could do. **Ivonne Gonzales Thompson** – for making the Spanish text flow better and critical clarity.

Ruth Schwartz, Erika Barrera-Camacho and her daughter Aiyana – for fresh proofreading eyes at the very end.

Genro Sato – for the scanning and image-processing work late at night, and for listening to me ramble on about this or that during the very long process required to make a book like this. You were there 100% of the time. I love you. Thank you!

Lastly, to my coauthors, **Kiyoshi and Kotomi** – who helped to both enrich and simplify the story with their unique perspectives as children. I couldn't do this creative work without you, sweeties. You're precious in all ways!

THANKS TO OUR EARLIEST SUPPORTERS

Sofia Colón

Virginia Winblad

Judy Rodriguez

Charissa Godfrey

Theresa Jones

Neverest Solutions, LLC

Deena Disraelly

Milagros Victoria Cepeda

Wilson Lee

Karl Wieser

Miyoko Hikiji

Gini Fiero

Marcela Gutierrez

Daniel Perry

Caroline Avakian

Laura Edwards

Christy Schultz

Lynette Hoy, Firetalker PR

Federico Subervi, Ph.D.

Eugenia Miranda

Brenda Herivel

Ikuko Sato

Douglas Woodford

Irene Chaparro

Marie Gagnon

Stacia H. Cragholm

Christine Walwyn

Angelica Perez-Litwin Ph.D.

Angelica Garcia

Miriam Hernandez

Cammie Herbert

Martha Hernandez

Stephanie Broyles

Melanie Wild

Akemi Furuyama

André Hill

Teachers from the 6th ESC-20 Dual Language Conference, San Antonio:

Julia Chapa

Marcy D. Voss

Clarissa Dovalina

Cecilia Canales

Irene T. Garcia

Veronica Bunton

Irma Herrera

Reba Siero

Kerrissa Torres

Kerrin Torres-Meriwether

Noriko Sato

Luz M. Rebollar

Caitlin Rice

Dan Sychr

The Funderburks

Lorena Clark-Gonzalez

Tina and Arturo Tiscareño

Lorenzo E. Agbenyadzi Padro

Meredith and Quint Nelson

Dawne Abdul Al-Bari

Sherry Bega

Luna Sophia Thomas

Mary and Alberto Lens

Diana Albarrán Chicas

Lisa Katzman

Irma Castañeda

Stephanie Gardner

Yvette Kurano

Sharman Asendorf

Endorsements

"…invites the reader into the world of Air Force aviation. Graciela writes this story in such an entertaining, exciting, and fun way that I wanted to be a KC-135 pilot after reading the book!"

—*Marcy Voss, Boerne ISD Special Programs Coordinator*

"…a wonderful sequel to *Good Night Captain Mama*. Graciela has crafted a story that blends military aviation, engineering and career opportunities while on a classroom field trip….Captain Mama inspires students of different ethnicities and genders, as well as English language learners, to possibly pursue careers in aviation."

—*Karla Orosco, Science Teacher at Admiral Akers Elementary, Naval Air Station Lemoore in Lemoore CA*

"My daughters really enjoyed the book; they immediately started discussing which character each would be on the crew."

—*Dali Rivera, Vetpreneur*

"I love how the author not only describes the duties of the individual officers, but she also includes an activity at the back of the book to extend the learning after the reading is done…a wonderful tribute to the Latinas who have and currently serve our country."

—*Monica Olivera, Creator, MommyMaestra.com*

"This bookshelf gem beautifully weaves adventure and storytelling, taking us onboard for an exciting insider's view of an aerial fueling plane…gender empowerment elements were equally as inspirational to me as to my children."

—Angelica Perez-Litwin, Ph.D., Founder, Latinas Think Big and CEO, Think Big Society, LLC

Critica de Libro

"*La Sorpresa de Capitán Mamá,* al igual que su predecesor *Buenas Noches Capitán Mamá*, es el cuento idóneo para compartir con nuestros hijos porque les enseña que sus madres son capaces de ser líderes en campos no tradicionalmente pensados para mujeres. De este modo el cuento también imparte un mensaje de igualdad de facultades de género."

—*Bloguera Victoria Cepeda, LatinasAllied.com*

"…una historia que mezcla la aviación militar, la ingeniería, y las oportunidades de carrera durante un día de excursión escolar…Más importante aún, Capitán Mamá inspira a estudiantes de diferentes nacionalidades, género y razas al igual que a los aprendices del idioma inglés, que pueden seguir carreras en la aviación."

—*Karla Orosco, Maestra de Ciencias en Admiral Akers Elementary, Estación Aérea Naval Lemoore en Lemoore CA*

"Esta maravilla de historia combina la aventura y la narración…Siendo narrado por un niño joven, somos testigos del momento especial cuando el niño explora el lugar de empleo de su Capitán Mamá. La mezcla de elementos de género nos ha dado inspiración a mí y a mis hijos."

—*Angelica Perez-Litwin, Ph.D., Fundadora, Latinas Think Big y CEO, Think Big Society, LLC*

"No creo que haya ningún otro libro para niños que destaque específicamente las Latinas dentro del servicio militar, lo cual hace tan valiosa esta serie…Adoro como la autora no solamente describe los deberes de cada oficial, sino que también incluye una actividad en la parte de atrás del libro para extender el aprendizaje después de que se haya terminado la lectura."

—*Monica Olivera, Creadora de MommyMaestra.com*

CPSIA information can be obtained
at www.ICGtesting.com
Printed in the USA
JSHW032243010621
15430JS00005B/28